Dog Gone

To my friends

A Doubleday Book for Young Readers
Published by
Random House Children's Books
a division of
Random House, Inc.
New York

DOUBLEDAY and the anchor with dolphin colophon are registered trademarks of
Random House, Inc.

Visit us on the Web! www.randomhouse.com/kids
Educators and librarians, for a variety of teaching tools, visit us at www.randomhouse.com/teachers

Library of Congress Cataloging-in-Publication Data

Harvey, Amanda.
Dog gone : starring Otis / Amanda Harvey.
p. cm.
"A Doubleday Book for Young Readers."
Summary: Otis is not happy being left at the Misty Meadow dog hotel,
but after running away, he is happy to find his way back.
ISBN 0-385-74639-3 (trade) — ISBN 0-385-90870-9 (lib. bdg.)
[1. Dogs—Fiction. 2. Kennels—Fiction.] I. Title.
PZ7.H26745Dof 2004
[E]—dc21
2003007837

The text of this book is set in 19-point Truesdell.
Printed in the United States of America
March 2004
10 9 8 7 6 5 4 3 2 1

Dog Gone

Amanda Harvey

A Doubleday Book for Young Readers

Last week I went to stay at the Misty Meadow dog hotel.

When we got inside, I noticed the other dogs watching me.
They looked friendly, but this place didn't feel much like home.

I was thinking I might not stay after all
when Lucy kissed me and said, "See you soon, lovely Otis."

Then she left.

Without me.

I watched day turn into night

and wondered how soon "soon" would be.

The next day, when the other dogs went out to play,
I remembered a story Lucy had read me.

It was about two dogs and a cat who made their way home
across a wild and unknown countryside. I could be a dog like that.

Straightaway, I set off.

Leaping over thorny hedges.

Swimming across dangerous rivers.

Racing through herds of woolly beasts. All on my way back home.

But which way was that?

Left or right? North or south?

I headed into the woods.

It was dark in there, and I seemed to be going in circles.

When I found a way out, I didn't know where I was.

I let out a small whimper. This had been my worst idea ever.

Then I spotted the woolly beasts, the dangerous river,

the thorny hedge, and the gate.

And Misty Meadow. Wonderful Misty Meadow.

I soared through the hoop.

I howled at the moon.

I devoured a late-night snack.

Before I knew it, Lucy was there,

and it was time to say goodbye.

I just hope my new friends
are at Misty Meadow the next time I stay over.